Prophecy: A Message to Humanity

Rowan Knight

Published by 22 Lions Bookstore, 2015.

Table of Contents

Title Page

Prophecy: A Message to Humanity
By Rowan Knight
Copyright © Rowan Knight, 2019 (1st Ed.) All Rights Reserved.
Published by 22 Lions Bookstore and Publishing House

About the Publisher

About the 22 Lions Bookstore:
www.22Lions.com
Facebook.com/22Lions
Twitter.com/22lionsbookshop
Instagram.com/22lionsbookshop
Pinterest.com/22lionsbookshop

Introduction

There are moments in life in which logic doesn't seem to match any possible expectation and what happens can be seen both as normal as well as surreal, and yet, out of an abnormal reality, we think about something that can't be possibly accepted because, if true, spreads mass panic, and, if not, leads us to ridicule.

25 of January 2013 was the day the mysterious reflected on my life, showing a man that could have been me from another time period. If logic is made out of the reality we usually feel, then that's when our reality changes to guide us into a new paradigm of observations.

As I was sitting and observing the French girl, a few tables away from me, writing compulsively in her napkin, I knew that it's not as much important understanding why she didn't even look at my face as to why was she writing in a napkin. But truly intriguing is the conversation that follows between two men. One of them is me and the other I have no idea of who can he be. And that's why this description, even though sharing information about a very realistic and probabilistic future for mankind, a future we should know, can never go beyond a personal speculation.

Chapter One - A Coffee in Paris

I am in Paris, on the 25 of January of 2013, and it's a very cold day outside, even though not raining. Something inside me tells me that I should be alone, so I follow my instinct and go to a coffee shop nearby that my gut guided me into.

There are moments in life in which logic is made out of the reality we usually feel and that's when our reality changes to guide us into a new paradigm of observations.

As I sit and observe the cute French girl, a few tables away from me, writing compulsively on her napkin, I know that it's not as much important understanding why she didn't even look at my face, as to why is she writing on a napkin. Strange people with strange behaviors, I must say. But not as strange as the ideas that come to me when I don't have a notebook to write them down.

The waiter approaches and I order an espresso, despite being lunch time already. I wasn't hungry but waiting with my laptop for the body to tell me when was time to eat. I checked YouTube for the first time in months, after moving to Communist China, where the most populated country in the entire world can't even access porn websites. I wonder what would happen to the world if they could.

As I immerse myself in distractive thoughts, a man entered, wearing a cap like mine; and I noticed, after ordering my espresso, that he couldn't stop looking at me.

His hair was white and his face quite old and innocent, but also very awkward, as if he had come from another century, maybe a time-machine that sent him to the future to make people like me wonder about the meaning of their present. Even though his appearance is mature and his eyes quite deep and sharp, I couldn't stop feeling him as someone quite strange. Something inside me was telling me that he just didn't belong there.

Nevertheless, this is Paris, where the weirdoes of the entire world can go to feel normal again, at least once in their lifetime. And I did meet many people like him before. But couldn't stop starring at this man, even though I did try to not get noticed. As a matter of fact, many people have described me in similar ways, even though I can't recognize it when seeing myself in the mirror.

I was just trying to respect his privacy as I often wish that people would respect mine. I'm tired of traveling to Switzerland, Turkey and Portugal and be treated like a Muslim Terrorist. At least in France they treated me with dignity, I believe, and surely, thanks to the amount of muslims living there. And yet, were these reflections of what we see or observations of what we wish to see? Mysterious is the mind of the mysterious man, and even more it is when he believes in his heart that his normality is unique in an insane world.

This man, in front of me, was dressed in black and wearing two medals in his chest — each with symbols I couldn't recognize, even with all the years I have in studying in the most unique religious societies.

He started looking at me and avoiding it when I looked back at him. But once his drink came, he approached me:

— "May I sit here?", He asked, while pointing at my table.

— "Sure!", I answered, not quite sure of what to say.

I had no reason to refuse. And he went straight to the point:

— "Are you who I think you are?

I guess he couldn't have started in a worse manner, because I've always wanted to believe that people often stare at me because I look different and not because they can recognize me. Destiny has its own away, and I wanted to know what this time it had to offer me, so I decided to maintain my honesty with this man and proceeded with the conversation.

Chapter Two - Two Men in Black

Here we were, two men dressed in black, with a black hat from the past century, in a coffee shop in the middle of Paris, in plain twenty-first century, seeming like we knew each other for a very long time, dressing the same and looking like twins. But I was feeling more lost than the owner of that establishment, wondering with his eyes about what could we possibly be talking.

— "Yes!", I answered to his question, not having, in fact, any choice to lie about.

— "I read one of your books! Very interesting indeed!", he continued.

— "Oh, that's nice!", I replied with a sarcastic tone, somehow between surprise and indifference. I was more curious about what would come next and not really interested in any recognition.

As he looked at his watch, not surprised at all with my lack of emotional feedback, continued:

— "I don't have much time! I have to catch the train to Switzerland soon, but I want to share something with you, that may allow you to write another book!", He said, in a tone that made me feel somehow apprehensive and watchful, as I felt that he wasn't completely being honest about his comment.

— "Please, continue!", I said calmly, not knowing if I should really care about it.

I've had many strange experiences in my life and it's not the first time that someone like him tries to attack me and even kill me, so I learned to have the cold blood of a snake and the instinct of a wolf in dealing with such people.

— "Thailand...!", He started, making me feel now that it was going to be just another lunatic sharing his crazy ideas, looking for some promotion through me. But what I was about to listen next went much further than what I could ever expect, changing me in a significant manner.

— "...That's where they've learned to control the body in order to control the mind; because, in order to know how to command, you must learn to obey, and that's how they've transferred what they've seen being done to baby elephants to human beings; that's the source of Pavlov's studies; Then, those who don't obey, are discriminated and pushed to exclusion and criminality."

— "Wow!", I reacted, feeling like my brain had just been smashed against a wall.

I had to find a way to control the conversation, though.

— "Please, help me understand better what you're talking about, so that I may know how to write it down for a book."

— "Sure! Allow me to continue!", He persisted. — "Purpose is being cause over life, and purpose is also making a human being become effect of a circuit or system. So, here we come to religion, which promotes effect as being something good; obeying as being good, disobedience as being bad and identity as something unacceptable; but it also teaches us about our social status, and the roles we play, as being something wonderful. Insanity, therefore, becomes something that occurs whenever a person accepts that he is a victim of his fate and refuses any responsibility over it."

— "Please continue!", I added, completely lost about the whole thing, but knowing that soon I would understand what he was trying to pass unto me.

— "If we promote the ability to develop a creation and make the human mind able to do so, memory and mental health improves; so creativity is suppressed from education. You can't think outside the predictable paradigm anymore when such thing happens. You can't say the unacceptable, you can't dream or imagine. If you start dreaming and being imaginative, you can't pay attention in a classroom and medicine is given to you to suppress that behavior furthermore."

— "What are you talking about?", I asked, while feeling frustrated for not being able to see the whole picture of his explanation.

— "It takes more than one lifetime to control a person to the level of insanity in which he has no more control over himself, and even your reaction can be traced to the same source. You see, the concept of open-minded is a person able to go beyond his bubble of psychological slavery, but when people believe that they are open-minded and then justify it with a perspective inside the bubble, they increase the effects of the system on them", He explained.

PROPHECY: A MESSAGE TO HUMANITY

While moving his arms apart, as if he was going to slap my face to wake me up from my feeling of numbness, he then raised his voice:

— "That's why it's cool to be stupid, it's cool to take drugs, it's cool to be sexually promiscuous, it's cool to believe in certain things, while following what they're supposed to follow. It's cool to follow a certain paradigm that defines coolness. It's cool to be popular by following ahead of the masses what the masses already believe. And so, my friend, the cool person, the leader, is the biggest puppet of them all. And...", He stopped, moved closer to my face, lowered his voice, clearly taking the attention of the three persons near us, and proceeded: — "...And he does the greatest job of all! He's the slave-king of slaves and believes to be part of the elite, believing that he's a VIP, famous, open-minded. But...", And he didn't gave me any chance to interrupt, I thought. — "...But all he is, represents the lowest level of the hierarchy; and that's why they suffer more from depression than anyone else. They are more insane than anyone else; and they depend on that insanity to be alive. And that's why they're so special to the real elite, hiding in the darkness of their souls. They're the demons that humans fear the most."

He stopped for five-seconds, stared at my eyes, and finished his explanation:

— "We worship demons; not movie stars or singers and writers."

— "Well, tell me something I don't know already", I told him, feeling now bored.

Chapter Three - How the World is Fooled

I tried to end this conversation, as it seemed like this man was imagining most of what he was saying.

— "People tend to replicate what they believe and they believe in what they see."

He pointed the finger at me, while slowing his voice and said:

— "Television is the greatest weapon against freewill and individual determinism, because it stops people's ability to dream and imagine a new world while hypnotizing them with a world of competition, aggression and anger, trapping them in the most primitive thoughts, just like Pavlov wanted. That's what Freud and Pavlov really gave us through their theories. Now, we all want relieve from those emotions, we want to forget those strong images, so we work harder and fornicate more. That's what they gave us, animalistic attitudes to make us undeveloped in just a few years, taking from us what took millions before to develop. And then they say that the law of attraction doesn't exist, and you wrote well about it in your books, but you don't know that when humans do believe in it they end up using it to make the system stronger, by attracting more money and more sex, better relationships, stronger families, happiness within an insane world, and, in the root of such vast system of branches, providing stability within something that shouldn't be stable."

He then touched my arm with his firm hand, to make sure I would listen and continued:

— "A spiritual jail... the law of attraction is being given so that humans can use all their new spiritual potential in this Age of Aquarius to learn to appreciate their spiritual jail. So, the law of attraction was allowed, not suppressed, to increase mass insanity. Although, when used adequately, it serves to demand from a god, from a victim's perspective, which is even worse. Eventually those poor people around us fail in applying the law of attraction because they can't get out of the paradigm, the jail they're in; and so, they can't attract something apart from what they can accept, and that's the mystery within this law, as it's now being refused and rejected by the masses that once accepted it. Those that still follow it got richer and more powerful. They got the relationships they wanted. But are they more spiritual? Oh, no! They didn't get it! They used it to reinforce their spiritual jail. This happens because the law of attraction is a consequence and not a cause of creation. If you believe, you achieve, but if your beliefs are given, your achievements are still predictable. You're not free! You may even become financially free, but you're still a slave in mind. And you say then that, "The Law of attraction made me achieve my dreams", and one day you die, everyone else receives those dreams and you reborn again, not remembering the knowledge, and within the same karma level that you haven't learn to overcome. And you forget that wonderful experience of being rich and you're born poor again, because you didn't understood what made you poor in the first place. You have changed one life, not the spirit in its eternal manifestation."

Chapter Four - How We Manifest Our Future

I had to ask for a glass of water, as I felt that it was too much information to absorb, even if I was really interested in the conversation. I tried to create a balance here, to make sure the old man wasn't misleading me:

— "For anything to happen you need to consent it first."

— "Yes, and you consent the bad in your life when you accept it as normal and predictable; and you also consent the good in your life in the same way. The more you visualize something as possible, the more possible it becomes. You create your life with willingness", He said, while making me feel like he had read it from my books and imagined the rest in his mind.

— "I think I wrote about that!", I told him, while allowing him to see that I wasn't trusting his words anymore. But he persisted:

— "You must allow a person to help you destroy hate, but if people aren't allowed to help, then hate for one another is increased. People want to destroy who they can't help. Therefore, the elite promotes help as being destructive, selfish or with the purpose of stealing, to diminish the willingness to receive help or increase the danger of helping someone that may betray us; and every time we're betrayed, that belief increases. But we can't see help anymore, because we lose the ability to recognize it, and we grow being selfish and with the concept of help as being associated with betrayal. We help in achieving something, to destroy someone,... and in doing so, we lose our life purpose, because if we can't help others, we can't feel joy in being alive. That's how depression comes to us. Depressive people reject help and can't really help anyone. People kill and steal when they can't work, they get angry and make revolutions when they can't work, because that's how they help society. A little child will go insane without the ability to help his parents. So, what are the governments really doing by supporting the conspiracy to destroy world economy? They're creating unemployment, to promote revolutions, which then destroy systems through the people themselves, so that later on they can present a solution that those same individuals will welcome as a better one, even though it was predicted all along. People want jobs, money to support their family, and much more. So, the government presents a solution for that, by giving them an alternative world in which they don't need money, but only a chip, and their work is supported with credits. The more they do, the more credits they get. Work or, in other words, help, pays-off, and people are again very happy with their governments, while using a microchip that allows controlling all their movements. With this solution in hand, the governments take on with their plan of controlling the population at distance, monitoring their thoughts and actions. Criminality decreases, happiness increases, while all along, the world becomes more inside a system of slavery without knowing it. Thoughts and emotions are monitored, controlled and manipulated, and that's the supreme form of slavery we will eventually have. With this implementation, something similar to what happens in Communist China may start occurring in a massive scale, with an inquisition taking on selective targets that oppose this order, starting naturally with the religious orders, especially the ones that promote rebellion and refusal in cooperating with such plan."

Chapter Five: The End of the World

I was surprised with his level of knowledge, and had to ask:

— "How do you know all this?"

— "Can't you see?", He asked baffled. — "I come from the future to deliver you this message, because there isn't much time left. I already knew that you would be here today, in this same coffee shop. I was waiting for you already when you arrived."

— "How could you possible know that? I am a nobody in this world?", I asked him confused about his words.

— "No, my friend, you are not", He answered, while adjusting himself in his sit and reclining backwards. — "Not now, at least! But you are a writer, and writers have power in their words. You will change this world with your books, and I know it. That's why I am here. You see, I am you. That's why I knew you would be here today. Because this date will be written in the book you will publish about our conversation."

— "But how will I change the world?", I asked.

— "One way or another, you will be famous. And I am using the extreme amount of reputation that you will gain in the future, to change the past. Because I was given permission to do so. And maybe, just maybe, you will lose your popularity by publishing my words and changing the world, but at least, you will sacrifice your own fame for the future of mankind."

— "Why is this so important?", I continued asking, not knowing the importance of my role by writing a book about this conversation. And he said:

— "After all these changes, there will be something called the Council of Foreign Relations and Inquisitions. And, as in the past centuries, with the Catholic Inquisition, this group will start annihilating many people. And that's when the real catastrophe begins, for we will lose many artists, writers, and thinkers in general. The world will become a very sad place to live for anyone. We will even lose the freedom to think, create and have opinions."

— "When will this inquisition take place and where?, I asked him now, while trying to know more, but it seemed that I had lost my chance to ask the right questions, for he looked at his other watch, as he took it from inside the pocket, before answering me whatsoever, and it seemed to me, unless I was not well in my brain, that this other watch he had, was running in another speed, not normal at all.

Chapter Six: A Final Thought

As he grabbed my hand, replied peacefully:

— "I'm sorry my friend, but I really have to go now", and upon saying this, waved at the waiter for the bill, paying both mine and his.

I didn't know what to say next, and before I had a chance to say whatsoever, he touched my shoulder and said his goodbyes:

— "It was nice talking to you my friend. And please trust yourself, because I know you can become me, as I once was you."

With these final words, I realized he was really me, even though I couldn't recognize it before.

I kept still, thinking about what he had just told me, truly a lot in a short period of time, while he put his black hat on and went away with a smile on his face and maximum description.

After that, I finished my coffee, and went for a walk near Notre Dame. And then I saw many police cars and one helicopter patrolling the area. Coincidence? Were they looking for my friend? I guess I will never know. But I did proceed to Switzerland after that day.

The many suspicious watching eyes I felt once arriving in Bern, made me believe that I was not welcomed. But I had never been there before. Or was why? Was it because my face was known? Or was it because I looked like my grandfather, a former spy in Switzerland that died without ever telling anyone the truth about who he was working for or where his fortune was hidden? Whatever could be the reason that made me feel uncomfortable with such behavior, probably attributed to racism, I finished the next three days in a small and quiet village near Bern, feeding ducks and cats in my spare time and relaxing my mind.

I never saw that man again, and I wondered if I did travel to Switzerland, but in a different time period. I wondered as well if I would return to France in the future to meet myself in this past. I was wondering if he was, in fact, me.

I guess I could have shared this story with other people, but little could they understand or believe.

I decided that it is much better, for my privacy and the mind of others, that I write this story and publish it as fiction. And that's what I did during those peaceful days in the Swiss village.

Book Review Request

Dear Reader, Thank you for purchasing this book! I would love to know your opinion. Writing a book review helps in understanding readers and also has an impact on other reader's purchasing decisions. Your opinion matters. Please write a book review! Your kindness is greatly appreciated!

Booklist

Books written by the author:
Agne: Inside the Mind of a Narcissist
Destiny: When Your Soulmate Finds You
Disenchanted: Poems by Rowan Knight
Illusion: When a Nymphomaniac Falls in Love
One Chance: 20 Short Stories with a Plot Twist and Moral Lesson
Prophecy: A Message to Humanity
Slave: Fulfilling a Prophecy
Soulless: Letters to a Narcissist

About the Publisher

This book was published by the 22 Lions Bookstore.

For more books like this visit www.22Lions.com.

Join us on social media at:

Fb.com/22Lions;

Twitter.com/22lionsbookshop;

Instagram.com/22lionsbookshop;

Pinterest.com/22LionsBookshop.